T0025283

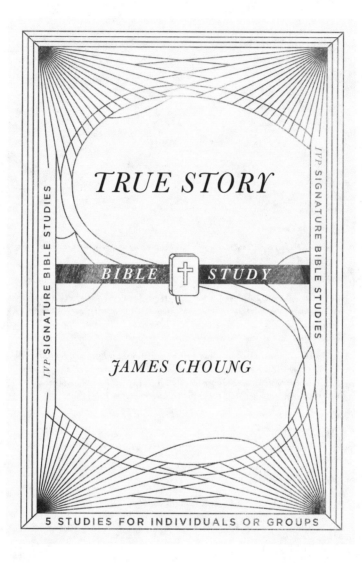

TRUE STORY

BIBLE ✝ STUDY

JAMES CHOUNG

IVP SIGNATURE BIBLE STUDIES

5 STUDIES FOR INDIVIDUALS OR GROUPS

An imprint of InterVarsity Press
Downers Grove, Illinois

InterVarsity Press
P.O. Box 1400, Downers Grove, IL 60515-1426
ivpress.com
email@ivpress.com

©2022 by James M. Choung

All rights reserved. No part of this book may be reproduced in any form without written permission from InterVarsity Press.

This study guide adapts material from True Story, *©2008 by James M. Choung.*

InterVarsity Press® is the book-publishing division of InterVarsity Christian Fellowship/USA®, a movement of students and faculty active on campus at hundreds of universities, colleges, and schools of nursing in the United States of America, and a member movement of the International Fellowship of Evangelical Students. For information about local and regional activities, visit intervarsity.org.

All Scripture quotations, unless otherwise indicated, are taken from The Holy Bible, New International Version®, NIV®. Copyright © 1973, 1978, 1984, 2011 by Biblica, Inc.™ Used by permission of Zondervan. All rights reserved worldwide. www.zondervan.com. The "NIV" and "New International Version" are trademarks registered in the United States Patent and Trademark Office by Biblica, Inc.™

While any stories in this book are true, some names and identifying information may have been changed to protect the privacy of individuals.

The publisher cannot verify the accuracy or functionality of website URLs used in this book beyond the date of publication.

Cover design and image composite: Autumn Short
Interior design: Daniel van Loon
Images: couple sitting on a bench: © Bruno Melo / unsplash.com
  colorful sky photo: © Dewang Gupta / unsplash.com

ISBN 978-0-8308-4660-3 (print)
ISBN 978-0-8308-4876-8 (digital)

Printed in the United States of America ∞

InterVarsity Press is committed to ecological stewardship and to the conservation of natural resources in all our operations. This book was printed using sustainably sourced paper.

Library of Congress Cataloging-in-Publication Data
A catalog record for this book is available from the Library of Congress.

P 24 23 22 21 20 19 18 17 16 15 14 13 12 11 10 9 8 7 6 5 4 3 2 1

Y 42 41 40 39 38 37 36 35 34 33 32 31 30 29 28 27 26 25 24 23 22

CONTENTS

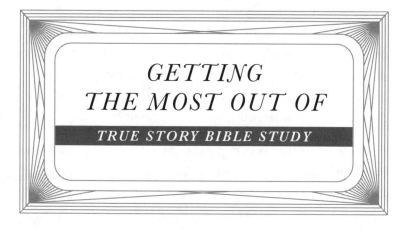

GETTING THE MOST OUT OF

TRUE STORY BIBLE STUDY

KNOWING CHRIST is where faith begins. From there we are shaped through the essentials of discipleship: Bible study, prayer, Christian community, worship, and much more. We learn to grow in Christlike character, pursue justice, and share our faith with others. We persevere through doubts and gain wisdom for daily life. These are the topics woven into the IVP Signature Bible Studies. Working through this series will help you practice the essentials by exploring biblical truths found in classic books.

HOW IT'S PUT TOGETHER

Each session includes an opening quotation and suggested reading from the book *True Story*, a session goal to help guide your study, reflection questions to stir your thoughts on the topic, the text of the Bible passage, questions for exploring the passage, response questions to help you apply what you've learned, and a closing suggestion for prayer.

The workbook format is ideal for personal study and also allows group members to prepare in advance for discussions and record discussion notes. The responses you write here can form a permanent record of your thoughts and spiritual progress.

Throughout the guide are study-note sidebars that may be useful for group leaders or individuals. These notes do not give the answers, but they do provide additional background information on certain questions and can challenge participants to think deeper or differently about the content.

WHAT KIND OF GUIDE IS THIS?

The studies are not designed to merely tell you what one person thinks. Instead, through inductive study, they will help you discover for yourself what Scripture is saying. Each study deals with a particular passage—rather than jumping around the Bible—so that you can really delve into the biblical author's meaning in that context.

The studies ask three different kinds of questions about the Bible passage:

* *Observation* questions help you to understand the content of the passage by asking about the basic facts: who, what, when, where, and how.

* *Interpretation* questions delve into the meaning of the passage.

* *Application* questions help you discover implications for growing in Christ in your own life.

These three keys unlock the treasures of the biblical writings and help you live them out.

This is a thought-provoking guide. Each question assumes a variety of answers. Many questions do not have "right" answers, particularly questions that aim at meaning or application. Instead, the questions should inspire readers to explore the passage more thoroughly.

This study guide is flexible. You can use it for individual study, but it is also great for a variety of groups—student, professional, neighborhood, or church groups. Each study takes about forty-five minutes in a group setting or thirty minutes in personal study.

SUGGESTIONS FOR INDIVIDUAL STUDY

1. This guide is based on a classic book that will enrich your spiritual life. If you have not read *True Story*, you may want to read the portion recommended in the "Read" section before you begin your study. The ideas in the book will enhance your study, but the Bible text will be the focus of each session.

2. Begin each session with prayer, asking God to speak to you from his Word about this particular topic.

3. As you read the Scripture passage, reproduced for you from the New International Version, you may wish to mark phrases that seem important. Note in the margin any questions that come to your mind.

4. Close with the suggested prayer found at the end of each session. Speak to God about insights you have gained. Tell him of any desires you have for specific growth. Ask him to help you attempt to live out the principles described in that passage. You may wish to write your own prayer in this guide or a journal.

SUGGESTIONS FOR GROUP MEMBERS

Joining a Bible study group can be a great avenue to spiritual growth. Here are a few guidelines that will help you as you participate in the studies in this guide.

1. Reading the recommended portion of *True Story*, before or after each session, will enhance your study and understanding of the themes in this guide.

2. These studies use methods of inductive Bible study, which focuses on a particular passage of Scripture and works on it in depth. So try to dive into the given text instead of referring to other Scripture passages.

3. Questions are designed to help a group discuss together a passage of Scripture in order to understand its content, meaning, and implications. Most people are either natural talkers or natural listeners, yet this type of study works best if all members participate more or less evenly. Try to curb any natural tendency toward either excessive talking or excessive quiet. You and the rest of the group will benefit!

4. Most questions in this guide allow for a variety of answers. If you disagree with someone else's comment, gently say so. Then explain your own point of view from the passage before you.

5. Be willing to lead a discussion, if asked. Much of the preparation for leading has already been accomplished in the writing of this guide.

6. Respect the privacy of people in your group. Many people share things within the context of a Bible study group that they do not want to be public knowledge. Assume that personal information spoken within the group setting is private, unless you are specifically told otherwise.

7. We recommend that all groups agree on a few basic guidelines. You may wish to adapt this list to your situation:

   a. Anything said in this group is considered confidential and will not be discussed outside the group unless specific permission is given to do so.

   b. We will provide time for each person present to talk if he or she feels comfortable doing so.

    c. We will talk about ourselves and our own situations, avoiding conversation about other people.

    d. We will listen attentively to each other.

    e. We will pray for each other.

8. Enjoy your study. Prepare to grow!

SUGGESTIONS FOR GROUP LEADERS

There are specific suggestions to help you in the "Leading a Small Group" section. It describes how to lead a group discussion, gives helpful tips on group dynamics, and suggests ways to deal with problems that may arise during the discussion. With such helps, someone with little or no experience can lead an effective group study. Read this section carefully, even if you are leading only one group meeting.

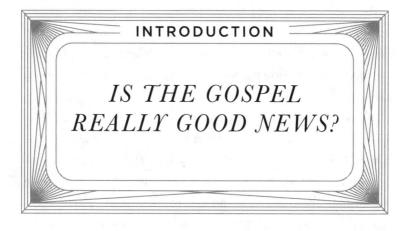

IS THE GOSPEL REALLY GOOD NEWS?

GOOD NEWS IS NOT MEANT TO BE HELD BACK. We're wired to tell someone about it. Whether it's a good book, an inspiring movie, a job promotion, a luxurious getaway, a catchy song, an exhilarating hike, or a random encounter with an old friend, we really can't wait to grab someone and load them up with the details.

So why is it so hard for us to share the greatest news in the history of humankind, the news that Jesus heals and restores our relationships with God, each other, and the rest of the world? One possibility: it doesn't feel like good news to us, and we worry that it won't sound like good news to our friends.

It's easy to be afraid of coming off as irrelevant, offensive, exclusionary, and closed-minded when talking about the gospel. And these days no one wants to be closed-minded. Sharing our faith can feel like putting ourselves in front of the firing squad of shame and rejection. We deal with enough of that in everyday life—why add more? It's demotivating: Why share a message that will draw scorn and ridicule? Ultimately, we don't really feel like we have good news to share. At least, not to them. Or maybe not even to us. That makes me wonder if we really have what Jesus taught in the first place. When he taught it, it must've felt like good news—to his followers and to the crowds who listened to him.

While we shouldn't water down the message just to say what others want to hear, we do want to share what Jesus came to teach. So what exactly did he teach? What was his central message? Shouldn't we share that with our friends? Jesus' message is about so much more than most of us realize, and it seems right to share the good news he came to offer.

Peter says in 1 Peter 3:15 that Christians should "always be prepared to give an answer to everyone who asks you to give the reason for the hope that you have." My intention is that this Bible study will help you understand a simple tool so that, when the occasion arises, you can share the hope that we have—one worth believing in.

For more insight, read "Before We Start" in *True Story*. Each session in this guide begins with an excerpt from the narrative sections of *True Story*, but you should also read the recommended passages from the book to get the full context.

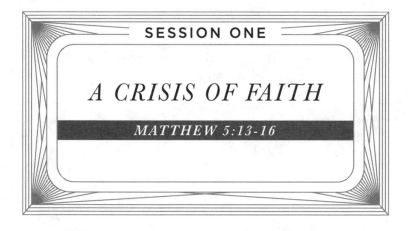

"**What good is Christianity** if it makes people like that?" Anna said. "What good is any religion if it just makes them angry, critical, and narrow-minded?

"Christianity's just another screwed-up religion! Seriously, what has Christianity done for us—or the world for that matter? They're just a bunch of hypocrites. That's what I think! Are they good for anything?" At the word *good*, her hands hit the table with a thud that drew the glance of the other customers.

She glared at Caleb while wiping away tears, waiting for a reply. Long seconds ticked away. He exhaled hard and shrugged his shoulders, saying the only truthful thing he could at the time.

"I don't know," Caleb said. "I just don't know."

SESSION GOAL	**READ**
Understand the need for a broader gospel.	Prologue of *True Story*

⟫⟫⟫ REFLECT ⟪⟪⟪

✳ Think of something *great* that happened to you in the past month. What was it? Who did you tell about it?

✳ How do you think your friends who are not Christian would respond to the gospel? Why?

⟫⟫⟫ STUDY ⟪⟪⟪

READ MATTHEW 5:13-16.

¹³You are the salt of the earth. But if the salt loses its saltiness, how can it be made salty again? It is no longer good for anything, except to be thrown out and trampled underfoot.

¹⁴You are the light of the world. A town built on a hill cannot be hidden. ¹⁵Neither do people light a lamp and put it under a bowl. Instead they put it on its stand, and it gives light to everyone in the house. ¹⁶In the same way, let your light shine before others, that they may see your good deeds and glorify your Father in heaven.

> "Various scholars have emphasized different uses of salt in antiquity, such as a preservative or an agent regularly added to manure; but the use of salt here is as a flavoring agent: 'if salt has become tasteless' (the Greek word can also mean 'become foolish,' so it may include a play on words)."*

1. What does it mean to be the "salt of the earth"?

2. What kind of "flavor" could Christians bring to the world?

3. How do irreligious people you interact with view Christians today?

4. In what ways have Christians become "tasteless"?

5. What does it mean to be the "light of the world"?

> "Jewish tradition considered Israel (Is 42:6; 49:6)
> and Jerusalem (as well as God and the law)
> the light of the world."[†]

6. If wicker oil lamps were common in Jesus' day, what would happen if you put a light under a bowl? Why might we put our light "under a bowl" today?

7. In what ways can we let our light shine so that others will glorify God?

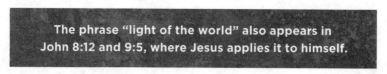

The phrase "light of the world" also appears in John 8:12 and 9:5, where Jesus applies it to himself.

8. What makes it difficult to let our light shine today?

———≋ **RESPOND** ≋———

✳ What kind of "flavor" do you feel led to bring to the world?

✳ How would you like to let your light shine before others?

———≋ **PRAY** ≋———

Ask God to help us keep our saltiness and brightness, particularly in our witness to the world.

---

*Craig S. Keener, *The IVP Bible Background Commentary: New Testament*, accordance electronic ed. (Downers Grove, IL: InterVarsity Press, 1993), 57.
†Keener, *IVP Bible Background Commentary: New Testament*, 57.

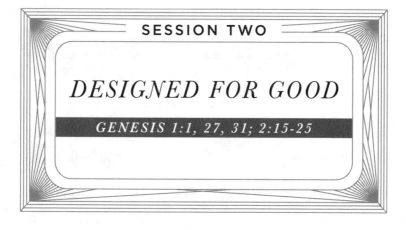

DESIGNED FOR GOOD

GENESIS 1:1, 27, 31; 2:15-25

"WE ALL ACHE—GROAN—FOR SOMETHING MORE, don't we?" said Caleb. "You said it perfectly: the world shouldn't be this way. If that's true, then that should point to something. I mean, our hunger points to something out there that should satisfy it—food. Our thirst points to something out there that should satisfy it—water. And our loneliness points to our need for relationships. So, shouldn't there also be something out there to satisfy the craving for a better world?

"There was once a world or there will someday be a world that's like that—a just one where there are right relationships all around. In the Christian worldview, as you remember, there was such a place. It was the way the world was at the beginning ..."

SESSION GOAL	READ
Glimpse an understanding of God's good design for the world.	Part one of *True Story*

═══◥ REFLECT ◤═══

✳ What is the world like today? What do you see on the news?

✳ How do you *feel* or *think* about how the world is doing?

═══◥ STUDY ◤═══

READ GENESIS 1:1, 27, 31; 2:15-25.

1 ¹In the beginning God created the heavens and the earth.

²⁷So God created mankind in his own image,
in the image of God he created them;
male and female he created them.

³¹God saw all that he had made, and it was very good. And there was evening, and there was morning—the sixth day.

2 ¹⁵The Lord God took the man and put him in the Garden of Eden to work it and take care of it. ¹⁶And the Lord God commanded the man, "You are free to eat from any tree in the garden; ¹⁷but you must not eat from the tree of the knowledge of good and evil, for when you eat from it you will certainly die."

¹⁸The Lord God said, "It is not good for the man to be alone. I will make a helper suitable for him."

¹⁹Now the Lord God had formed out of the ground all the wild animals and all the birds in the sky. He brought them to the man to see what he would name them; and whatever the man called each living creature, that was its name. ²⁰So the man gave names to all the livestock, the birds in the sky and all the wild animals.

But for Adam no suitable helper was found. ²¹So the Lord God caused the man to fall into a deep sleep; and while he was sleeping, he took one of the man's ribs and then closed up the place with flesh. ²²Then the Lord God made a woman from the rib he had taken out of the man, and he brought her to the man.

²³The man said,

"This is now bone of my bones
and flesh of my flesh;
she shall be called 'woman,'
for she was taken out of man."

²⁴That is why a man leaves his father and mother and is united to his wife, and they become one flesh.

²⁵Adam and his wife were both naked, and they felt no shame.

1. God described creation as "very good" (1:31). Describe a time when you felt something you created was good. Why did you consider it good?

2. In verse 27, both men and women are made in God's image. What does that say about the value of who we are?

> "In the ancient world an image was believed to carry the essence of that which it represented. . . . In Mesopotamia a significance of the image can be seen in the practice of kings setting up images of themselves in places where they want to establish their authority."*

3. What in creation did God consider "not good" (Genesis 2:18)? Why?

4. What's happening in verses 2:19-20? What does this show about who God is?

5. How did Adam feel about his new helper?

> In Hebrew, the word *helper* is a compound word, meaning both "to save" and "to be strong." It doesn't have the meaning of subservience we give it today. It's used twenty-one times in the Old Testament—seventeen times of God, and is he weaker than us? The female helper was meant to save with strength, making her important and powerful.

6. What was the relationship between Adam and his wife (Genesis 2:25)?

7. What could that kind of relationship look like in our relationships today?

Everything was made to be a source of good for
everything else: a land of mutual blessing, a people
of mutual blessing, and a faith of mutual blessing.

8. In what ways is creation, as you see it, good?

RESPOND

＊ When God created the world, he designed it for good. In
what ways could you display more of God's image in your life?

＊ Since we are all made in God's image, what are ways you
could honor that image in yourself and in others?

⋙ PRAY ⋘

Take time to thank God for the good things he has made—in the world, in our relationships, and in each of us.

---

*John H. Walton, Victor H. Matthews, and Mark W. Chavalas, *The IVP Bible Background Commentary: Old Testament*, accordance electronic ed. (Downers Grove, IL: InterVarsity Press, 2000), 29.

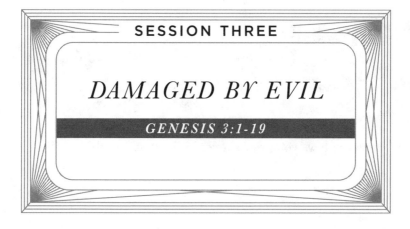

"**BUT PEOPLE WEREN'T SATISFIED,** even in this good place," said Caleb. "We didn't like taking orders, and we definitely didn't want someone else to have leadership over our lives, even if that someone else was far better qualified to run the place. Instead, we wanted to run this ship—this world—as captains. We wanted to be in charge, to take the Designer's place. We were going to live for ourselves and bend everything in creation to serve our own purposes and pleasures. . . .

"Even if I stop doing wrong things, I don't love people around me the way I should. You're right: we're all screwed. That's how we get a world like this. Look around. Evil. Everywhere. All around us and all in us. We've been left unchecked and need some resources to help fight against the system, against others who are oppressing. We even fight ourselves; we don't often do what we know we should."

"So," said Anna, "you're saying that I might also be a part of the problem and might not even know it?"

<table>
<tr><td>

SESSION GOAL

Explore the extent of the damage
and evil in us, with us, and around us.

</td><td>

READ

Part two of *True Story*

</td></tr>
</table>

REFLECT

✳ What have you grieved over in the past month?

✳ What in our world would you call damaged or broken?

STUDY

READ GENESIS 3:1-19.

¹Now the serpent was more crafty than any of the wild animals the LORD God had made. He said to the woman, "Did
God really say, 'You must not eat from any tree in the garden'?"

²The woman said to the serpent, "We may eat fruit from
the trees in the garden, ³but God did say, 'You must not eat
fruit from the tree that is in the middle of the garden, and
you must not touch it, or you will die.'"

⁴"You will not certainly die," the serpent said to the
woman. ⁵"For God knows that when you eat from it your

eyes will be opened, and you will be like God, knowing good and evil."

⁶When the woman saw that the fruit of the tree was good for food and pleasing to the eye, and also desirable for gaining wisdom, she took some and ate it. She also gave some to her husband, who was with her, and he ate it. ⁷Then the eyes of both of them were opened, and they realized they were naked; so they sewed fig leaves together and made coverings for themselves.

⁸Then the man and his wife heard the sound of the Lord God as he was walking in the garden in the cool of the day, and they hid from the Lord God among the trees of the garden. ⁹But the Lord God called to the man, "Where are you?"

¹⁰He answered, "I heard you in the garden, and I was afraid because I was naked; so I hid."

¹¹And he said, "Who told you that you were naked? Have you eaten from the tree that I commanded you not to eat from?"

¹²The man said, "The woman you put here with me—she gave me some fruit from the tree, and I ate it."

¹³Then the Lord God said to the woman, "What is this you have done?"

The woman said, "The serpent deceived me, and I ate."

¹⁴So the Lord God said to the serpent, "Because you have done this,

"Cursed are you above all livestock
and all wild animals!
You will crawl on your belly
and you will eat dust
all the days of your life.

¹⁵And I will put enmity
>   between you and the woman,
>   and between your offspring and hers;
>   he will crush your head,
>   and you will strike his heel."

¹⁶To the woman he said,
>   "I will make your pains in childbearing very severe;
>   with painful labor you will give birth to children.
>   Your desire will be for your husband,
>   and he will rule over you."

¹⁷To Adam he said, "Because you listened to your wife and ate fruit from the tree about which I commanded you, 'You must not eat from it,'
>   "Cursed is the ground because of you;
>   through painful toil you will eat food from it
>   all the days of your life.
>   ¹⁸It will produce thorns and thistles for you,
>   and you will eat the plants of the field.
>   ¹⁹By the sweat of your brow
>   you will eat your food
>   until you return to the ground,
>   since from it you were taken;
>   for dust you are
>   and to dust you will return."

1. In what ways did the serpent start to undermine Eve's trust in God?

"The serpent was not in every respect an ordinary animal. He was not 'craftier than' the other beasts of the field. Rather, he was crafty 'and the wild animals were not.'"*

2. What tempted Eve to take the fruit (Genesis 3:5-6)?

God always intended us to know the difference between good and evil. He'd already given us one command: Do not eat from this particular tree. People began to know what was good—in step with God's design—and what was not good—out of step with God's design.

3. Where was Adam when Eve took the fruit (Genesis 3:6)? What does this say about the responsibility for what happened there?

4. What does Adam's response in verse 10 show about how he was feeling in front of Eve and God? Why?

5. What were Adam and Eve doing in verses 7, 12, and 13? In what ways do we also do the same?

> In Genesis 3, Adam and Eve chose against the Designer. As a result they felt shame. Weird. Nothing changed on the outside—they were still naked as always. But now they knew they were naked. So they tried to cover themselves with leaves. We now have cycles of shame and blame.

6. What is the promise in the curse to the serpent (Genesis 3:15)?

7. What is the curse to Eve (Genesis 3:16)? What is the impact on gender relationships of all people contrary to their original design?

8. What is the curse to Adam (Genesis 3:17-19)? What is the impact on work and life, and how is this contrary to their original design?

⟋⟍⟍ RESPOND ⟋⟍⟍

✳ How is our relationship with the world and its systems damaged by evil?

✳ In what ways do we need to ask forgiveness for the ways we have contributed to the mess in the world?

PRAY

Confess—basically, acknowledge the truth—before God, and ask for forgiveness for the ways we contribute to the mess in us, in our relationships, and out in the world.

---

*Frank E. Gaebelein, ed., *Expositor's Bible Commentary* notes, 1st accordance electronic ed. (Grand Rapids, MI: Zondervan, 1990), paragraph 483.

RESTORED FOR BETTER

COLOSSIANS 1:15-23

"But didn't Jesus save me?" Caleb's voice was trembling.

"Well," said Shalandra, "yes—and far more. He not only saves us but the world. *Salvation* in the original language also means 'deliverance' and 'healing.' So we've been saved-delivered-healed from our sins, are being saved-delivered-healed from our sins, and will one day be finally saved-healed-delivered from our sins. So he saved you not only from eternal punishment, but also from the destruction your sin is causing you and the evil your sin is leading you into. Yes, he saved you—but not only from the punishment of your sins. He also saved you *from* your sins, and from sin itself. And he did this not only for you, but for the entire world."

"What do you mean by the world?"

She drew herself up. "I mean that Jesus didn't just save you and me. He saved-delivered-healed our relationships. He's doing the same with systems around us, like racism and materialism. He wants to do that with nations, governments, schools, churches, cultures. All of it can be restored for better."

SESSION GOAL	READ
Understand how Jesus restored all of creation for better.	Part three of *True Story*

REFLECT

✳ Think of something you owned that was damaged but is now restored. What did it take for the repairs to happen?

✳ When something is restored, what is its value compared to the original?

STUDY

READ COLOSSIANS 1:15-23.

¹⁵The Son is the image of the invisible God, the firstborn over all creation. ¹⁶For in him all things were created: things in heaven and on earth, visible and invisible, whether thrones or powers or rulers or authorities; all things have been created through him and for him. ¹⁷He is before all things, and in him all things hold together. ¹⁸And he is the head of the body, the church; he is the beginning and the

firstborn from among the dead, so that in everything he might have the supremacy. [19]For God was pleased to have all his fullness dwell in him, [20]and through him to reconcile to himself all things, whether things on earth or things in heaven, by making peace through his blood, shed on the cross.

[21]Once you were alienated from God and were enemies in your minds because of your evil behavior. [22]But now he has reconciled you by Christ's physical body through death to present you holy in his sight, without blemish and free from accusation—[23]if you continue in your faith, established and firm, and do not move from the hope held out in the gospel. This is the gospel that you heard and that has been proclaimed to every creature under heaven, and of which I, Paul, have become a servant.

1. What does it mean for the Son—Jesus—to be the firstborn over all creation (Colossians 1:15)?

> "'Firstborn' could refer to the position of authority and preeminence given to the firstborn son in the Old Testament (Gen 49:3-4). . . . This term could also refer to the redemptive role of the firstborn (cf. Col 1:14) or be another title for God's 'Son.'"*

2. What do verses 16-19 tell us about Jesus?

3. In Jesus, "all things" are reconciled back to God (Colossians
   1:20). List some kinds of "all things" that can be reconciled
   to God.

> Anything that was used for another allegiance
> can be realigned for God's good purposes. God
> was not just saving the people in the world;
> he was saving the world itself as well.

4. What was our status with God "once" (Colossians 1:21)?

5. What is our status with God after being reconciled?

6. Why is Christ's physical body important in the reconciliation (Colossians 1:20-22)?

> Paul could be "alluding to and answering 'the false spiritualism' of the Colossian heretics. Asserting that reconciliation could be accomplished only by spiritual (angelic) beings, they attached little or no value to the work of Christ in a physical body."[†]

7. What hope does this bring for us, our relationships, and our world if "all things" can be reconciled?

8. How do you think people who are saved can continue in faith
   and hope?

<div align="center">~~~⋙ <strong>RESPOND</strong> ⋘~~~</div>

✳ Name something that you desire to be reconciled to God
  through Jesus' blood shed on the cross.

✳ In what practical ways can we die and live in Jesus each day?

<div align="center">~~~⋙ <strong>PRAY</strong> ⋘~~~</div>

If you have not yet done so, commit your life to God, for you are
reconciled back to God through Jesus' death and resurrection. Ask
God to show you how he wants you to die and live again today.

---

*Craig S. Keener, *The IVP Bible Background Commentary: New Testament*, accordance electronic ed. (Downers Grove, IL: InterVarsity Press, 1993), 572.

†Curtis Vaughan, *Colossians*, in vol. 11 of *Expositor's Bible Commentary*, ed. Frank E. Gaebelein,
accordance electronic ed. (Grand Rapids, MI: Zondervan, 1978), paragraph 56467.

THE BIG STORY

Jesus preached, "The time has come. . . . The kingdom of God is near. Repent and believe the good news!"

In that short sentence Jesus summarized the gospel, and he preached on this subject more than any other topic in Scripture: more than the afterlife, sexuality, morality, marriage, money, or religious legalism. He spent most of his earthly ministry defining and describing the kingdom of God. This kingdom was marked by a new kind of people with a new kind of relationship with God and each other, living out a new kind of life—one that exuded love for God and neighbor. This love needed to be expressed through evangelism, world missions, social justice, financial stewardship, and vocational calling, among others. The kingdom of God was meant to heal the planet. To me, this finally feels like good news, not just for Christians but also for the world.

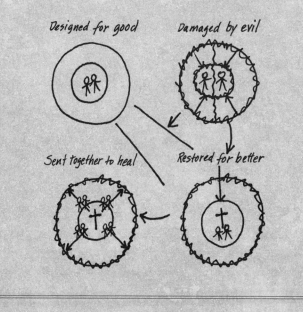

Designed for good

Damaged by evil

Sent together to heal

Restored for better

When I understood this, the splinter in my brain was out, but now I had a new problem. While understanding the gospel as "the kingdom of God is near" finally gave me a theology that could hold all the kingdom values together, it also became abundantly clear that the current gospel diagrams did not communicate the fullness of Jesus' statement. We needed something new.

The gospel needs to recapture the biblical story—what I call the Big Story. When sharing the gospel, we need to restore what's good about the Christian message to give hope and healing back to our family, our friends, and the world.

(Adapted from "Behind the Scenes" in *True Story*)

SENT TOGETHER TO HEAL

"Now we live in between those times," Caleb said, "between the start and finish of the restoration project. It's like we're in the middle of a construction project and we know what it'll look like in the end, but we're still dealing with the rafters, the wiring, the buttresses, the rubble—the mess. The resistance has started, but the revolution isn't complete. So evil still exists, injustice still happens, racism still works its evil through societies, oppression still continues. But we've also got glimmers of hope and places of victory . . ."

"So we fight for justice in the meantime?" said Anna. "I don't mind that at all."

"In the meantime, we all have our orders from Jesus to be sent out as operatives of justice and healing. We're being sent out together to heal this broken planet. Lots of Christians don't understand this and remain on the sidelines. But we don't go out in a paternalistic or imperialistic way either; we go in love and service. It's our role to make this world a better place. We start within ourselves, letting Jesus take the lead of our lives, training ourselves so that we're the kinds of people we wish to meet someday. We become the kinds of people who can—by the leading of God—do good instead of evil, love instead of hate, forgive instead of perpetrating injustice."

SESSION GOAL	READ
Know our place in being sent together to heal—for ourselves, each other, and the world.	Part four of *True Story*

REFLECT

✳ What, in your mind, should Christians be doing?

✳ What could Christian community look like as we engage each other and the world?

STUDY

READ MATTHEW 28:18-20.

[18]Then Jesus came to them and said, "All authority in heaven and on earth has been given to me. [19]Therefore go and make disciples of all nations, baptizing them in the

name of the Father and of the Son and of the Holy Spirit,
²⁰and teaching them to obey everything I have commanded
you. And surely I am with you always, to the very end of
the age."

READ ACTS 2:42-47.

⁴²They devoted themselves to the apostles' teaching and to
fellowship, to the breaking of bread and to prayer.
⁴³Everyone was filled with awe at the many wonders and
signs performed by the apostles. ⁴⁴All the believers were
together and had everything in common. ⁴⁵They sold
property and possessions to give to anyone who had need.
⁴⁶Every day they continued to meet together in the temple
courts. They broke bread in their homes and ate together
with glad and sincere hearts, ⁴⁷praising God and enjoying
the favor of all the people. And the Lord added to their
number daily those who were being saved.

1. The Matthew passage represents some of Jesus' last words to
   us while he was on earth. What does it mean that Jesus has
   "all authority" (Matthew 28:18)?

2. In the original language, "make disciples" is the main verb.
   "Going," "baptizing," and "teaching" all modify that verb.
   Why does it matter which one is the main verb?

From the very outset, Jesus invites disciples to join in
his mission—to advance the kingdom he started. He
wants them to look up from the selfishness of their
own hearts and to start serving others with love
and justice. "Come follow me . . . and I will send
you out to fish for people" (Matthew 4:19).

3. The Acts passage is a picture of early Christian community.
   What were some of the rhythms of this community?

4. How did the people within the community experience it?
   How could that be replicated today?

> We need the Holy Spirit and the community
> of Jesus' followers to help us in the fight. We
> can't do it alone. More importantly, we need to
> become the kind of good that we want to see on
> the planet. We need to be transformed so we can
> take evil full on and not be corrupted by it.

5. How did the people outside of the community experience it?

6. What could we learn about how to relate to people outside
of our community today?

> In Acts, we read multiple times that the church
> continued to grow as people from a variety of
> backgrounds responded to God's work and joined
> the community (see Acts 2:41; 4:4; 5:14; 6:1, 7).

7. In what ways does this community reconcile "all things"?

8. What keeps Christians from living like this today?

RESPOND

✳ In what concrete ways can you be a part of healing the world with Jesus and his community?

✳ Who would you like to share the gospel with? What would be your next steps to do that?

PRAY

If you don't have one, pray for a community of faith that can help you become the good you want to see in the world. Then pray for someone you know to be open to Jesus' good message, and begin to think about how you would share this message with that person.

LEADING A SMALL GROUP

LEADING A BIBLE DISCUSSION can be an enjoyable and rewarding experience. But it can also be intimidating—especially if you've never done it before. If this is how you feel, you're in good company.

Remember when God asked Moses to lead the Israelites out of Egypt? Moses replied, "Please send someone else" (Exodus 4:13)! But God gave Moses the help (human and divine) he needed to be a strong leader.

Leading a Bible discussion is not difficult if you follow certain guidelines. You don't need to be an expert on the Bible or a trained teacher. The suggestions listed below can help you to effectively fulfill your role as leader—and enjoy doing it.

PREPARING FOR THE STUDY

1. As you study the passage before the group meeting, ask God to help you understand it and apply it in your own life. Unless this happens, you will not be prepared to lead others. Pray too for the various members of the group. Ask God to open your hearts to the message of his Word and motivate you to action.

2. Read the introduction to the entire guide to get an overview of the subject at hand and the issues that will be explored.

3. Be ready to respond to the "Reflect" questions with a personal story or example. The group will be only as vulnerable and open as its leader.

4. Read the chapters of the companion book that are recommended at the beginning of the session.

5. Read and reread the assigned Bible passage to familiarize yourself with it. You may want to look up the passage in a Bible so that you can see its context.

6. This study guide is based on the New International Version of the Bible. It will help you and the group if you use this translation as the basis for your study and discussion.

7. Carefully work through each question in the study. Spend time in meditation and reflection as you consider how to respond.

8. Write your thoughts and responses in the space provided in the study guide. This will help you to express your understanding of the passage clearly.

9. It might help you to have a Bible dictionary handy. Use it to look up any unfamiliar words, names, or places.

10. Take the final (application) study questions and the "Respond" portion of each study seriously. Consider what this means for your life, what changes you may need to make in your lifestyle, or what actions you can take in your church or with people you know. Remember that the group will follow your lead in responding to the studies.

LEADING THE STUDY

1. Be sure everyone in your group has a study guide and a Bible. Encourage the group to prepare beforehand for each discussion by reading the introduction to the guide and by working through the questions for that session.

2. At the beginning of your first time together, explain that these studies are meant to be discussions, not lectures. Encourage the members of the group to participate. However, do not put pressure on those who may be hesitant to speak during the first few sessions.

3. Begin the study on time. Open with prayer, asking God to help the group understand and apply the passage.

4. Have a group member read aloud the introductory paragraphs at the beginning of the discussion. This will remind the group of the topic of the study.

5. Discuss the "Reflect" questions before reading the Bible passage. These kinds of opening questions are important for several reasons. First, there is usually a stiffness that needs to be overcome before people will begin to talk openly. A good question will break the ice.

   Second, most people will have lots of different things going on in their minds (dinner, an exam, an important meeting coming up, how to get the car fixed), which have nothing to do with the study. A creative question will get their attention and draw them into the discussion.

   Third, opening questions can reveal where our thoughts or feelings need to be transformed by Scripture. That is why it is important not to read the passage before the "Reflect" questions are asked. The passage will tend to color the honest reactions people would otherwise give, because they feel they are supposed to think the way the Bible does.

6. Have a group member read aloud the Scripture passage.

7. As you ask the questions, keep in mind that they are designed to be used just as they are written. You may simply read them aloud. Or you may prefer to express them in your own words.

   There may be times when it is appropriate to deviate from the study guide. For example, a question may already have been answered. If so, move on to the next question. Or someone may raise an important question not covered in the guide. Take time to discuss it, but try to keep the group from going off on tangents.

8. Avoid offering the first answer to a study question. Repeat or rephrase questions if necessary until they are clearly understood. An eager group quickly becomes passive and silent if members think the leader will give all the *right* answers.

9. Don't be afraid of silence. People may need time to think about the question before formulating their answers.

10. Don't be content with just one answer. Ask, "What do the rest of you think?" or, "Anything else?" until several people have given answers to a question. You might point out one of the study sidebars to help spur discussion; for example, "Does the quotation on page seventeen provide any insight as you think about this question?"

11. Acknowledge all contributions. Be affirming whenever possible. Never reject an answer. If it is clearly off base, ask, "Which verse led you to that conclusion?" or, "What do the rest of you think?"

12. Don't expect every answer to be addressed to you, even though this will probably happen at first. As group members become more at ease, they will begin to truly interact with each other. This is one sign of healthy discussion.

13. Don't be afraid of controversy. It can be stimulating! If you don't resolve an issue completely, don't be frustrated. Move on and keep it in mind for later. A subsequent study may solve the problem.

14. Try to periodically summarize what the group has said about the passage. This helps to draw together the various ideas mentioned and gives continuity to the study. But don't preach.

15. When you come to the application questions at the end of each "Study" section, be willing to keep the discussion going by describing how you have been affected by the study. It's important that we each apply the message of the passage to ourselves in a specific way.

   Depending on the makeup of your group and the length of time you've been together, you may or may not want to discuss the "Respond" section. If not, allow the group to read it and reflect on it silently. Encourage members to make specific commitments and to write them in their study guide. Ask them the following week how they did with their commitments.

16. Conclude your time together with conversational prayer. Ask for God's help in following through on the commitments you've made.

17. End the group discussion on time.

Many more suggestions and helps are found in The Big Book on Small Groups *by Jeffrey Arnold.*

SUGGESTED
RESOURCES

Based on a True Story
James Choung

The Challenge of Jesus: Rediscovering Who Jesus Was and Is
N. T. Wright

Colossians Remixed: Subverting the Empire
Brian J. Walsh and Sylvia C. Keesmaat

Kingdom Come: How Jesus Wants to Change the World
Allen Wakabayashi

Real Life: A Christianity Worth Living Out
James Choung

THE IVP SIGNATURE COLLECTION

Since 1947 InterVarsity Press has been publishing thoughtful Christian books that serve the university, the church, and the world. In celebration of our seventy-fifth anniversary, IVP is releasing special editions of select iconic and bestselling books from throughout our history.

RELEASED IN 2019

Basic Christianity (1958)
JOHN STOTT

How to Give Away Your Faith (1966)
PAUL E. LITTLE

RELEASED IN 2020

The God Who Is There (1968)
FRANCIS A. SCHAEFFER

This Morning with God (1968)
EDITED BY CAROL ADENEY AND BILL WEIMER

The Fight (1976)
JOHN WHITE

Free at Last? (1983)
CARL F. ELLIS JR.

The Dust of Death (1973)
OS GUINNESS

The Singer (1975)
CALVIN MILLER

RELEASED IN 2021

Knowing God (1973)
J. I. PACKER

Out of the Saltshaker and Into the World
(1979) REBECCA MANLEY PIPPERT

A Long Obedience in the Same Direction
(1980) EUGENE H. PETERSON

More Than Equals (1993)
SPENCER PERKINS AND CHRIS RICE

Between Heaven and Hell (1982)
PETER KREEFT

Good News About Injustice (1999)
GARY A. HAUGEN

The Challenge of Jesus (1999)
N. T. WRIGHT

Hearing God (1999)
DALLAS WILLARD

RELEASING IN 2022

The Heart of Racial Justice (2004)
BRENDA SALTER McNEIL AND
RICK RICHARDSON

Sacred Rhythms (2006)
RUTH HALEY BARTON

Habits of the Mind (2000)
JAMES W. SIRE

True Story (2008)
JAMES CHOUNG

Scribbling in the Sand (2002)
MICHAEL CARD

The Next Worship (2015)
SANDRA MARIA VAN OPSTAL

Delighting in the Trinity (2012)
MICHAEL REEVES

Strong and Weak (2016)
ANDY CROUCH

Liturgy of the Ordinary (2016)
TISH HARRISON WARREN

IVP SIGNATURE BIBLE STUDIES

As companions to the IVP Signature Collection, IVP Signature Bible Studies feature the inductive study method, equipping individuals and groups to explore the biblical truths embedded in these books.

Basic Christianity Bible Study
JOHN STOTT

How to Give Away Your Faith Bible Study
PAUL E. LITTLE

The Singer Bible Study, CALVIN MILLER

Knowing God Bible Study, J. I. PACKER

A Long Obedience in the Same Direction Bible Study, EUGENE H. PETERSON

Good News About Injustice Bible Study
GARY A. HAUGEN

Hearing God Bible Study
DALLAS WILLARD

The Heart of Racial Justice Bible Study
BRENDA SALTER McNEIL AND
RICK RICHARDSON

True Story Bible Study, JAMES CHOUNG

The Next Worship Bible Study
SANDRA MARIA VAN OPSTAL

Strong and Weak Bible Study
ANDY CROUCH